Ex Libris

# With Two She Flew

## Cathy Bodega

PARK END BOOKS

Sugar Land
2020

Cover design: Summer Kinard

Publisher's Cataloging-in-Publication Data

Names: Bodega, Catherine, 1995-, Author
Title: With Two She Flew
Description: Sugarland [Texas] : Park End Books, 2020.

Identifiers: ISBN: 978-1-953427-03-8
Subjects: Juvenile Fiction-Disabilities & Special Needs
Juvenile Fiction-Social Themes-Religion & Faith

Library of Congress Control Number: 2020918433


www.parkendbooks.com

For the little bird under my wing.

# one

Daisy Anastasia Burns was just like her pet dove Cooey. Every morning, Cooey sang his song and sorted his seeds. His favorite seeds, he left in the bowl to eat at his leisure. The ones he didn't like, he tossed onto the floor outside the cage.

When it came to her own feelings, Daisy had a harder time than Cooey. She could count them—2, 4, 7, 16 feelings at a time—but she could not see the patterns by herself. That's why Mommy made Daisy her own set of seeds. When Daisy was overwhelmed, she sorted her seeds.

She put her happy feelings into the veil of the Theotokos, the Mother of God, for safekeeping and her sad ones into Jesus' arms on the cross for Him to eleison. "Eleison" was a word for mercy and grace and healing. It was a big word that described the love of a big God who could handle her big feelings.

Daisy reached into Cooey's cage and stroked the soft feathers on his neck. The bird cooed and cuddled his face against her warm hand. She whispered to him, "Church today, Cooey. I'll look to see if the Holy Spirit looks like you today." She knew that God was all around them, but her eyes weren't good at always seeing God without help from the holy icons and the angels.

"The angels have wings like birds, except they're wings of fire," she whispered to Cooey. "I only see their faces sometimes, when they lean close." She leaned closer to Cooey and touched her nose to his soft head. "Angels smell like the wind in a rose garden. Their wings move the air in church."

Daisy filled Cooey's seed cup and washed and refilled his water vessel. She replaced them in the cage. "I'll be back," she said.

She ate her breakfast of oatmeal with maple syrup and a cup of chocolate milk. Her brothers were swinging in the soft, blue swings that hung from the kitchen doorways. Her parents were talking by the sink, and her baby sister was eating an apple slice by the back door. Daisy took a deep breath and smiled. She was a safe girl, snug in her nest.

She finished her oatmeal, which her sister called, "egg mail," and she took her bowl to the sink. "Look, Mom. I finished my egg mail. Can I go see Cooey again now?"

"Yes."

Cooey was sorting his seeds. He would need to fly around the living room later. Daisy could tell if Cooey needed a longer time out of his cage by how he threw his seeds out. Mom never understood how she knew. Mom looked at the numbers of the different types of seeds, but only Daisy saw the patterns. Daisy could tell that Cooey missed the sky today.

"I know, Cooey bird, but your weak wing makes outside unsafe."

Cooey cooed. Daisy felt... felt...felt overwhelmed.

She got out her seed cards and opened her sorting folder on the ground beside Cooey's cage. On one half of the folder was an image of the Crucified Lord with a space to tuck her sad seeds behind his outstretched arms. The other half was an image of the Theotokos holding out her veil of protection, with a space to tuck her happy seeds behind the veil. Mom had asked Daisy's best friend, Natalyia, to color the drawings for the board and seeds. They were filled with bright metallic accents just like Daisy liked.

She found the seed for sad and turned it till she could see the glittery dark blue squiggles on the seed shape. She gave it to Jesus. She found the seed

4

for wistful and thought, "Is wistful sad or happy?" It was both. She offered it to Theotokos, who always gave to her Son anyhow. She found "hope" and entrusted it to God's mother for safekeeping. She thought of how happy Cooey must have been flying above them before the neighbor's cat got hold of him. She gave "joy" to Mama Mary and "scared" to the Cross.

"Is that all, Cooey?" she asked.

Cooey fluffed his feathers.

Daisy added "safe" to the veil of the Theotokos. She had added birds around the edges of the drawing of the Protection of the Theotokos when she colored it. Mom had said it was okay to add to the edges of the pictures when she and Natalyia made the seed board the year before. Daisy traced the birds she had drawn flying toward the Mother of God and tucking their heads under their wings under the picture of the Crucifixion. Daisy had made all the birds gray under the Cross, because it had been dark that day.

Dark could be sad, but sometimes God made surprises in the dark, too. Sometimes there was Pascha in the dark.

Daisy thought of the candles and music of Pascha the week before when her whole church gathered to celebrate the Resurrection. She sang, "Come receive the Light that was never overtaken by night, and glorify Christ, who is risen from the dead." Cooey flapped his wings. He liked her singing. If she colored another seed sorting board, she would ask Mom if it was ok to give one of the birds a candle in the drawing.

Mom sat beside Daisy. It was almost time to leave for church.

"Daisy, it's time for shoes and hair brushing. Shoes first, then hair."

Daisy looked at her seed sorting. It was okay. She was okay. She closed up her prayers, tucking all of the seeds safely into the pockets of the prayer folder, and stood up. "Okay, Mommy." She fluttered her hands to her sides and stood on tiptoes. Mom called Daisy her little Bird Girl because of the way Daisy fluttered and flapped when she was happy.

The whole family got ready for church. When it was time to go, they gathered the church bags by the back door. Daisy held her church bag, and her big brother Gabe held the big church bag for the other children. Daisy looked in her bag to make sure she had everything: a little notebook, alphabet and bird stickers, a pencil, a soft dove hand puppet that Daisy hugged sometimes, and a visual schedule to help her know where they were in the service. Daisy added her seeds and seed sorting board. One of the babies had put a springy silicone bracelet and a St. Nicholas peg doll in her bag by accident. She handed the extra toys to Gabe to put in the big bag. On the drive to church, she cuddled her dove puppet.

When they arrived at church, the angel wings were faster and more fiery than usual. Daisy took three deep breaths to calm herself. There was a smell like metal making the air bitter almost as quickly as the beeswax candles sweetened it.

Something was wrong.

The family usually bought candles to light when they venerated the icons in the Narthex, but several extra men from the church stood around the candle box, blocking their view. Dad talked to them in low whispers. Daisy stared up at the wall of grownup backs. She couldn't understand what the men were saying. They spoke in Spanish, but they sounded angry. After a few minutes, Mr. Gonzales, the head usher, turned, patted Gabe's shoulder, and nodded. The other men nodded and stepped sideways to make a path for the family to get to the candles. A strange man stood behind the welcome desk. He started to say something to Dad, but Mr. Gonzales stopped him. Mom pulled Daisy to her side, and fire flashed in the wings all around them.

# two

"You excited about meeting your little friends here today?" The man was looking at Daisy.

"My daughter has autism," Mommy said to the stranger. "Leave her alone." Daisy wasn't used to hearing Mom sound so bossy except when she was telling the children to pick things up off the living room floor. Mom glared at the man, and Daisy heard the low crackle of warning in the air. Mommy was friends with the angels, and she was named after one of their leaders. Whatever Mom thought about this unwelcome man, it was clear that the angels shared her opinion.

The man nodded and looked away. "Just doing my job, Ma'am."

"You shouldn't be here. You shouldn't be in a church unless you came to pray." Dad put a hand on Mommy's arm, and Daisy saw a light like gold fill the air around them. Mommy dropped her shoulders. "I'll pray for you," she said to the man. "You pray for us, too, please."

The man nodded.

Mom kept Daisy tucked to her side as they went through the pattern of welcome. She kissed the image of Jesus as Lord of All and opened her eyes to God's power. She kissed the Theotokos holding baby Jesus, and she opened her eyes to God's love. She kissed the Gospel and opened her ears to God's teaching. She kissed the hand of the church's patron saint, St. Anastasia the Healer, and her hands found strength to lift her heart to the Lord.

Daisy liked to lift her heart. Daisy had been afraid the first time she recognized the words, but it didn't mean that anyone really took their hearts out of their bodies. Mommy had said we feel love in our chests because we are born with a built-in need for hugs. If there were a way to lift up her heart for real, she would be holding her arms up for a hug. Daisy closed her eyes and imagined her love and safety and joy and sadness and all of her feelings and seeds reaching out from the middle of her chest to outside herself, because even though she couldn't see God, God was right there, hugging her.

It wasn't too strange a thought if she remembered how many other things she couldn't see: babies before they were born, the rooms on the other sides of doors, the air she breathed, the songs she sang and the songs birds sing. She couldn't see where life came from or where it went, but it was there inside and all around like God and the air.

"Daisy?" Mom whispered. "Let's go to our seats." Daisy opened her eyes and looked around. She was still in front of the icon of Saint Anastasia the Healer. She might have been there for a few minutes, because there was a line behind her. It was okay to go into the church even though it was bigger enough, louder enough, and full enough of the strong scent of incense that she was overwhelmed. She didn't have to worry if she needed to close her eyes and cover her ears a little, because her eyes and ears stayed open to see and hear God even when she covered them. Even if she had to squeeze her sensory ball or touch her seeds, the saints could still hold her hands to get them ready for the God hugs.

In their seats, Daisy listened to the prayers for the whole world. She looked at the icons and smelled the incense that reminded her a little of the angels that said, "Peace," and she saw the lovely whole world connected by uncountable tiny strings of love and light, all pulling, pulling toward the cup that Father carried around the church as he sang for God to remember them all in God's kingdom.

Daisy said, "yes" in her heart and nodded "yes" when Father walked past carrying the whole world in a cup. She sang, "Amen" with the choir when Father took the world into the Royal Doors. She liked to watch the strings that pulled her into the altar, too.

She liked the way they glowed when Father said, "Lift up your hearts" and the people answered, "We lift them to the Lord" and tugged the strings so that God was among the people, and the people were in the altar, and everything in the world danced and sang.

It was too much to look at directly for very long, so Daisy mostly looked at her stickers and toys. Sometimes she played peek-a-boo with Rosie, her baby sister. Sometimes she helped her little brothers Nicky and Georgy find their pencils. No matter what else she did, though, she could see the glow and feel the tug of those thin, bright strings.

The service was almost to Daisy's favorite part, when they knelt down to sing, "We praise thee, we bless thee," and got up to sing to the Theotokos. She smiled as her friends Natalyia and Nicholas rushed in right between songs. They came to church with their mom and sat right by Daisy's family. They spoke Russian to her little brothers to make them smile and helped Dad when Mom had to take Daisy out for a calm down.

Today Natalyia had her hair in a pretty French braid. Daisy thought it was pretty as a crown. She nudged her big brother Gabe and whispered, "Natalyia's hair is a crown!" He didn't turn to her, so she pushed his leg with her foot to get his attention.

Suddenly, all the fiery wings flapped around them. Gabe's knee crumpled, and he nearly fell on top of Georgy and Nicky. He caught himself on a fiery hand and the back of the pew in front of him.

"Daisy!" he hissed, "You almost knocked me down!"

She didn't mean to. She looked at Natalyia's crown and the subsiding brightness in the faces around her. The light was backing away from the faces. She had chased it away. Her brother Gabe was her best friend. He was hurt. The babies! Her little brothers had been in danger. Mom looked scared. Dad held Nicky and rubbed Georgy's head. Rosie whined, "I want to hold you" in a sleepy voice at Dad's knee. Daisy wasn't sure if she could still breathe. She wasn't sure if she had feet, or if they had been frightened and run away without her.

Mom was pressing her shoulders. Suddenly her feet came back, and her ears hurt. Someone was yelling. "I didn't mean to! I didn't mean to!"

"Breathe, Daisy," Mom whispered, breathing deeply. "You're shouting. Let's go sort your seeds." Mom held up the seed folder with the photo of Cooey on the front. Behind Mom's head, the Holy Spirit fluttered like a dove over the waters of creation in the icon of the baptism of Christ. It was a new creation, a new dove.

Daisy took a deep breath, and the sound that had been hurting her ears stopped, leaving her ears bouncing to the drumbeat of her heart. She held Mom's hand and walked with her toward the calm down room at the back of the church. Natalyia's crown leaned down as Daisy passed by. She was telling Georgy and Nicky that it would be okay. Daisy heard her brothers try to repeat something in Russian.

On the way to the back, some of the people shook their heads with sharp eyes meant to punish her for her noise. But most people had soft faces like the marshmallows Mom gave Daisy when she had a sore throat. The sharp eyes and the soft eyes rippled behind a rainbow of fiery wings that surrounded Daisy and Mom.

They stepped into the Calm Room, and Mom gave Daisy the seed folder.

"Why are the wings so bright around us?" Daisy sniffled.

"Our guardian angels are fierce today. They are singing God's love so loudly that you can see it with your nous, the heart of your body and soul together."

Daisy sat and pulled out the seeds from the pocket. She picked out fear, remorse, joy, sadness, worry, love, awe, happiness, compassion, and curiosity. "Do you see with your nous, Mom?"

"A little, Daisy. God's love is like a room full of treasure I can only see a little, but I stumble into beauty everywhere I go. You were born with your spiritual eyes open. For you, the challenge is to not be afraid of what you see."

"What's your challenge?" Daisy asked. She put "love" onto the Cross.

"Mine is to be brave enough to see."

Daisy looked at the seed for "awe" and thought about the fire in the air.

"I'm going to help with the little boys now," Mom said. "You finish sorting, and then come back to sit with us."

# thRee

"Yes, Mom," Daisy said. She set "fear" into the care of the Cross. Should love stay there, or should she ask Theotokos to help with that? She put love on the Cross right next to fear. It seemed that love and fear were both alike in church.

Outside, the wind blew the azaleas against the windows of the quiet room. From the corner, an answering pop as soft as a falling seed sounded.

Daisy turned to look and saw a narrow crack opening in the wall. She stood and walked to the crack and leaned over and peeked in with one eye. It was a door, and a steep staircase ascended into the half shadows. She had heard about the ladder of divine ascent, and she wondered if maybe it had been opened to her just like in the stories Dad read to Gabe each Lent.

She walked up the first three steps and paused, looking for the saints that must be on the staircase with her. Another gust of wind outside pulled the hidden door closed behind her. The change brought quiet, but it was a little strange to have a real door on the heavenly ladder. She sat on the step and looked at the door. As far as she could recollect, the angels of God descended and ascended, but there wasn't generally mention of doors. There was a handle on this side. She thought of turning it and going back to her seeds. She supposed that she might after all have only found an ordinary staircase and not a heavenly one. Then the light came.

Above her, the sunlight poured through a stained-glass window of the Holy Theotokos of the Sign. She walked halfway up the stairs and held her face up in the rich red glow. She went up a few more steps, almost to the top of the flight. She closed her eyes and let the red and blue and golden light play over her eyelids as she slowly turned her head from side to side. The colors were like the sheltering wings that kept her safe. They were a glory that could touch her face and God's face at once. She breathed deeply and relaxed in the slow and steady heat of the stained-glass light on her face.

"What are you doing?" a small voice asked near her head.

Daisy thought at first that it was an angel, so she didn't jump. She opened her eyes and turned to look at the round little face just above her own. It was the face of a girl ringed in dark curls.

"I'm glorying in the light," Daisy said. "What are you doing?"

"Hiding."

Daisy nodded and walked up the remaining stairs. The little girl sat back, and Daisy saw that there were three little girls in all, all covered in the light from the Theotokos. She sat down next to them and stared.

"Who are you?" the little girl asked.

"I'm Daisy. I'm autistic."

"Was that you who was yelling?"

"Probably." Daisy shrugged. She thought of her seeds. She needed to get back to them soon. "But then the wind showed me that you are here."

"Then we're friends. My name is Hannan. Those are my sisters, Nour and Mary."

"I'm Daisy. Well, Anastasia in church. Daisy Anastasia. I only have one sister and three brothers."

The little girls stood slowly, silently, and walked closer to Daisy. They were like three little matushka dolls with matching dark brown hair and eyes, though their chins and faces were different shapes. Hannan was the middle girl, and she seemed to be about Daisy's age, though Daisy was taller. Nour was the littlest, not much older than Georgy and Nicky, and Mary must have been the same age as Gabe. They were dressed in simple, well-made cotton play dresses that Daisy recognized from the perpetual hand-me-downs passed to every family in the church. That made them her family. Her baby sister Rosie was wearing a dress from that same set of dresses, too.

Daisy smiled and remembered her manners. "What do you think of this place?" she asked. She pointed outside through a pane of glass that showed the courtyard and trees beyond the parking lot.

"We haven't seen trees like this in a long time," Hannan said.

Nour spoke up. "Mama and the other women were our trees in the camp."

"She means they held out their hands to pray," Mary explained, holding her hands out to her sides and lifting up a piece of heaven. There was an answering echo of light around the girls as the angels recognized the gesture.

"Every morning they swayed and sang, and God was the wind in their trees," Nour finished.

Mary started to explain again, but Daisy cut her off.

"I know what she means. I've seen it, too."

Mom's Society of St. Philaret meetings were like that, when all the women stood, tall and short together, to pray for the poor and the sick.

"Nour has inside eyes," Mary said. "She talks about the things of her heart. Mama said we'll help her here to say normal things."

"I don't know how to say normal things, either," Daisy said to Nour. The smaller girl's eyes were as deep as a spring. Cooey would like her, because she would remind him of the sky. "But it's safe here to have inside eyes," she said to Mary.

"Dad said it would be," Hannan whispered, and the wings around the four girls flashed fierce and protective as a father's prayer. "He said we could be safe here to love poetry and beauty, and no one would blow it to shreds." Her lips quivered, and fat tears came.

Mary patted her sister in the way big sisters patted – not like a mother, but so you remembered that you had a mother and that she loved you. It was the way that Daisy touched Rosie when she was telling her about Cooey. It was how she patted Cooey when she told him about the sky.

Daisy nodded. "I talk to birds," she said.

"Do they talk back?" Nour asked.

"Sometimes."

Nour smiled.

In the church below, the choir sang, "We have seen the light, the true light," and Daisy smiled. "I have to go back now," she told Hannan.

"Will you come back?"

"Yes." Daisy ran down the stairs and closed the door shut so that it was invisible in the wall.

# fouR

Back in the calm down room, Daisy bent and sorted her seeds quickly, putting everything onto the cross. She kissed the Theotokos and the Cross and closed her folder just in time before Mom came in the main door.

"All better, baby girl?"

Daisy nodded. "I missed communion, but can we come back tomorrow for St. George's Day?"

"Yes, Daisy. We can come back tomorrow. Are you ready for Sunday school?"

Gabe poked his head in the door. "Come on, Daisy. I got you some antidoron," he said, handing her a piece of blessed bread. "Let's go to class." It was their first week back at class since Pascha, and they missed their friends.

Mom kissed the top of Gabe's head. "Thank you for getting your sister. Come get me in the St. Philaret's meeting if she gets upset again." Mom turned to Daisy and knelt to her level. "I'm taking the little ones to their class with Dad. I'll be in the conference room." She kissed Daisy's forehead. "You're a safe girl," she whispered. "You're my little Bird Girl with God in her heart."

Daisy stood on her tiptoes and fluttered her hands by her side. She liked when Mom told her she was safe. If she was safe, her questions were, too.

She ate the little piece of blessed bread that Gabe held out to her and followed him through the long hallway to the classroom for older elementary kids. Gabe saw his friend and sat by him across the table. Daisy sat next to Natalyia in a chair close to the door. The teachers walked in carrying trays of juice and snack bars.

Ms. Jocelyne sat the juice down and said, "Ok, everyone. Stand up and make your cross." While they were shuffling to stand, Ms. Elena quickly served 10 sets of snack bars and napkins, one set for each child. Ms. Elena made her cross and nodded to Ms. Jocelyne. They began to say the Our Father together, and Daisy was happy that she didn't stumble over any of the words this time.

When they had sat back down, Ms. Elena asked, "What did you notice that was different in church today?"

Now was Daisy's chance to ask about the strange man and the hidden girls. She wasn't sure they were related, but they were both different. She decided to ask about the man first, but she wasn't sure which hand to raise. She looked at Natalyia to see if she was going to ask, too. Natalyia always picked the right way to do things, and Daisy could learn from her.

Natalyia raised her right hand. "We sang the Christos Anesti."

"That's right," Ms. Elena said.

"Let's sing it now," Ms. Jocelyne added. She opened the wall cabinet to reveal the words to the hymn written out in English and the Spanish with pronunciation marks. Everyone stood again and sang.

When they were seated again, Ms. Elena began to pass out coloring sheets of the Resurrection icon. Daisy knew they would move to the lesson quickly, so she had to act now.

Daisy raised her right hand.

"Yes, Daisy?" Ms. Elena asked. Her voice was softer because she knew that Daisy didn't like loud.

"Why was there a strange man at church today? Mom didn't like him."

The teachers looked at each other with tight lips. Daisy saw their eyebrows dip in anger, but they must not have been angry at Daisy for asking. When they looked at her, they were sad. "The men in church are here to try to find some of our parishioners they're chasing. They followed the family to church on Pascha and think they'll come back soon."

Daisy looked around the room at her classmates. Johnny hadn't been to church in a long time because of his soccer schedule. "Is it Johnny's family? Are they chasing him because he got back from soccer?"

"No, Daisy," Ms. Jocelyne said. Her voice was strained as though it was hard for her to stay quiet. "They're chasing my sister and brother-in-law and their daughters, my nieces. They want to send them back into the war they escaped." Ms. Jocelyne swallowed hard and wiped at her eyes with the back of her hand.

Daisy froze. She had hurt Ms. Jocelyne like she had hurt Gabe. Her heart flew into the bars of her ribs. Natalyia reached out and held her hand.

"Daisy, breathe," Natalyia said. "Daisy, breathe with me, okay?" Natalyia breathed giant gulps of air and blew them out loudly. "Come on. Let's pick our favorite colors for Jesus' robes." Daisy loved coloring with Natalyia. Natalyia would fill in tiny, perfect dots and diamonds on the robes of the saints, and Daisy would color around them. The teachers always asked if they could hang the girls' pictures on the wall for everyone to see.

Daisy looked at the coloring pages that were taped in neat rows along the wall next to her. She joined Natalyia in a deep breath. Then she saw taped to the wall the picture of the Three Holy Children in the Fiery Furnace. Natalyia had brought a special gold ink pen that day, and they had worked extra hard to make it beautiful. The colors were rich and vibrant as the ones that poured on Hannan, Nour, and Mary from the window in their hiding place. Daisy shook her head.

"I'll take her," Natalyia said. She stood and led Daisy by the hand to the conference room door. "Go on in and find your mother. I'll do the details on the picture and give it to Gabe so you can finish the colors at home." Natalyia hugged Daisy lightly and walked back towards their class.

# five

Daisy took a deep breath and opened the door. One of the older women was speaking. "-if we can't get a hard cast for Susan's arm." She stopped suddenly when she heard the door close behind Daisy. Nineteen sets of mother eyes looked Daisy over. Her godmother, Marina, said, "Hey, there, sweetie. Lock the door behind you and come sit with your Nouna."

Daisy locked the door and went to Nouna Marina. Marina was only a head taller than Daisy, but she had the loudest voice. She was a lawyer who helped people in courts. She scooted over so that Daisy could sit on half of her chair. Then she nodded to the old woman who had been speaking. "Go on," she commanded in her mismatched voice.

Daisy hid herself behind Nouna Marina's big, curly hair as the older women whispered and shot looks in their direction.

"Well," a young woman spoke up, "we don't have to be at the hospital for that part. I can get her to the ER for X-rays without the agents seeing her. I can do the cast back at," she paused to look at Daisy, "the place where Susan is."

The old woman who had spoken before sniffed loudly and wiggled her nose. Daisy knew that meant she was annoyed with Daisy being there. Usually when they were annoyed, people thought children were going to mess up their plans or find out things they shouldn't know yet.

"Is Susan the name of Hannan's mommy?"

Mrs. Helen who ran the church bookstore leaned around Nouna Marina and asked, "Who's Hannan, Daisy?" in a sweet voice.

"Hannan and Mary and Nour are in the secret room. The strange man is trying to catch their whole family, and Ms. Jocelyne started crying."

Mrs. Helen shot a look to her cousin Efi, who walked quickly out of the room towards Daisy's class. The other women looked at Mom, who had been watching Daisy and her Nouna quietly from across the table. Mom frowned and leaned forward. "Daisy, have you told anyone about those girls?"

Daisy shook her head. "No, Mom. The wind showed them to me and made us friends, and I told them I would come back." She told her mother what had happened in class. Suddenly, Daisy was enveloped in the smell of a warm field of flowers. Nouna's soft, strong arms were around her, and her voice boomed over Daisy's head, "My goddaughter is so smart. She came right to us. Now, ladies, let's get these agents out of our church so we can get those girls back with their parents."

The women began to talk back and forth, some in Spanish and some in English, in the rapid-fire way that people settled plans when they knew what they were talking about. They reminded Daisy of the tree women who sheltered her new friends with their prayers. She let herself let go of each little word, until the women's voices were the wind in the trees, the only sign of the hidden wind that moved the world.

Mom tapped Daisy lightly on the shoulder. "Daisy, honey, will you be our helper?"

Daisy blinked and looked around. The women were quieting. Several had already gathered their bags and papers and stood. The young doctor who had spoken about the cast gave Daisy a thumbs up sign as she pulled on her jacket. Mom tapped Daisy again.

"Daisy, we want you to sort your seeds every Liturgy until we can get these agents removed. Do you think you can do that?"

Daisy tucked her head towards her Nouna's arm again. "Do you mean, because I'm too loud?"

"No, Daisy. Because you're the bravest girl we know. And because they've seen you go into that room before to calm down. They won't follow you."

Daisy thought of her friends in their little nest. They were bird girls like her, and bird girls stuck together. "Yes, Mommy. I'll do it!"

A couple of women jumped, and Nouna Marina squeezed her and said, "That's my goddaughter with the strong voice like her Nouna!" Mom smiled.

"Thank you, Daisy."

# SIX

The family skipped coffee hour. Mom said it was so that "everyone could have a quiet afternoon to recover from a long day." Daisy knew that meant that Mom wanted Daisy to be able to use all of her sensory strategies to regulate so she could feel safe and happy again. She wasn't sure what she thought about Mary and Hannan and Nour in their little nest feathered with angel's wings and chased by hunters. She had too many feelings at once, and she was glad Mom and Dad decided to leave after Sunday school.

Her heart danced in her chest on the short drive to their tall house with its own little copse of woods to the side. Sometimes the angels were taller than the trees, and sometimes they were as small as a cloak around her shoulders. Today they seemed to be everywhere, calling just under her hearing, "Fear not! Fear not!" in cadence with the birdsong in the trees.

As soon as Mom opened the minivan door, Daisy rushed inside to finish her after church chores. She prepared five sippy cups of sweet iced tea. She handed four of them to her brothers and sister and took the last one with her to the living room. She sat next to Cooey's cage to fill him in about the girls in the nest at church. Talking to Cooey reminded Daisy of Nour.

"I met a girl today who will be your friend. Her eyes know the hope of skies, and they are as deep as the water under the earth. Do you remember in the beginning, Cooey? How God separated the waters above the firmament and the waters beneath the firmament? She's got eyes that remember all that water and all that sky, like you."

Cooey rubbed his head on Daisy's finger and made a low, "coo-coo."

"I will tell her you want to see her." Daisy smiled. "She'll like that. She ran away from a place where the sky was falling, just like you."

"Daisy?" Mom asked from the doorway into the kitchen, "Good. You have your drink. Bring it to the table, please. It's time to eat your macaroni and cheese."

"Yes, Mom." Daisy hopped up from the floor beside Cooey's cage. "I'm finished with the biggest part of my news anyway."

"Daisy yelled a lot in church today," Gabe said. "Was it because of the agents in the halls?"

Daisy was chewing, but she made a small, scared sound.

"You're safe, Daisy," Gabe bossed. "I just need to know if that's what the big deal was. Why are they there anyway? They scared my little sister and made Ms. Jocelyne cry."

"Hmm," Daisy said, relieved. She had thought she had made Ms. Jocelyne cry.

"They're chasing the Georges because they think they can get away with detaining them without cause and taking their belongings." Dad spat the words out as though they were salt in his sweet iced tea. "They're here legally, but some troublemaker decided not to look into that little detail. They want to catch the family and deport them out of pure venom."

"Well," Mom added, "It's possible that the men at the church are just following orders, but they're bad orders. They aren't supposed to chase people into churches. The trouble is, they're already abusing their powers by chasing legal immigrants. Our church has lots of legal immigrants, so we have to hide the family until we can get them away from the church safely and with legal protection from other parts of the law."

"How is there more than one law?" Gabe demanded.

"Oh, law!" Nicky interrupted. "Oh, laws!" He mimicked his Sunday school teacher, a plump woman with a Southern accent who often said, "Oh, laws" and "Lawd, have mercy!" The other babies giggled and joined in. They repeated their joke and turned it into a chant.

"Oh, laws!" shouted Georgy, Nicky, and Rosie in unison. They broke down into giggles, until little bits of their macaroni and cheese dribbled out of the corners of their grins.

"Okay, babies. That's enough," Mom said. "Gabe, the immigration agents have certain leeway to act that aren't due process. But if we can keep Susan and Bassel and the girls away from the agents until we have court orders in place and all of their immigration paper work on their persons with lawyers present, we can help them live their lives here the way they're supposed to be able to."

Daisy watched as a saint stepped forward and placed his hands-on Mom and Dad's shoulders. She stared at the space where he waved like a concentrated patch of air and light until she recognized his kindness. St. Joseph the Betrothed, who had carried baby Jesus to safety. Mom and Dad looked at each other across the saint's hands. Their faces relaxed.

"But you children don't need to worry," Dad said. "Be brave, but don't worry. We're all going to work together to take care of our church family."

"You mean St. Joseph is helping, too!" Daisy said. She could hear him now, whispering in her heart and into her parents' hearts. "Be brave, but don't worry." Like all saints' voices, his echoed wherever she moved. Mom nodded and smiled at Daisy.

"Yes, Daisy. Exactly. We've asked St. Joseph's help before every meeting. What a surprise that you made that connection!"

"It's not hard when he's right here, Mom," Daisy said.

"What's he saying, Daisy?" Gabe asked. He liked to know when Daisy could hear the saints. They would read saint stories and prayers together and wonder what they would sound like if they were less weird and old-fashioned.

"Be brave, and don't worry."

Dad nodded. "That's right, Daisy." He smiled at Mom again.

"Oh, laws!" Rosie shouted into the quiet.

"I'm going to be very brave," Daisy yelled over the babies' giggles. "I'm going to make sure no one finds the girls in the nest!"

"What is she talking about?" Dad asked Mom.

"I'm going to sort my seeds during Liturgy so the bad men don't get my friends."

"Wait a minute. You're going to --Gabriela, did you know about this?" Dad looked shocked. "No. She can't do that." He shook his head. "We can't put that on her. She's a child. We can't ask her to do that."

"Eve and Charlotte thought she would be the perfect deterrent. You know how loud Daisy can be when she gets overwhelmed."

Dad shook his head. "She's autistic. What's she going to think if we reward her for screaming in church?"

"It's not a reward!" Daisy shouted. "I don't do it on purpose! I'm not going to start doing it on purpose! Just to help Nour, and then I'll stop UNLESS I CAN'T HELP IT!" Daisy burst into angry, confused, ashamed tears. "I didn't mean to, Daddy!" she cried.

Then Daddy's beard was pushing her hair away from her left ear, and he was hugging her close. He stroked her shoulders and sang in his deep, lilting voice. "Safe girl. Safe girl. Safe girl. Daisy is my safe bird girl." She caught her breath in jagged gulps and listened to Dad. He sang to her as though he was chanting in church, and Daisy felt her heart calm just as it did when all those strings lifted up. "I'm sorry, Daisy. I was worrying instead of being brave. You're my little girl, and I love you. If you want to help by sorting seeds, you can try again. But tomorrow, let me try something else first."

Daisy nodded. When she spoke, her voice was like birdsong compared to the low rumble of air and water in Daddy's song. "What are you going to try? Are you going to sort your seeds?"

Dad laughed and hugged Daisy around the shoulders, careful not to squish her waist. He knew that she felt squeezed instead of hugged if anyone put pressure below her shoulders. "No, Daisy. Tomorrow I'm going to lock the door."

# seven

The cardinal woke Daisy early the next morning. She supposed he had heard some news.

"Yes, cardinal," Daisy said, "It's St. George's Day. And my friends are in a nest at church." She blinked slowly as the cardinal chirruped. Then she remembered what her mother had said at yesterday's lunch. "It's my friends' feast day, in a way. Their last name is George." She turned onto her belly and propped herself on her elbows. "Cardinal, do you have a feast day, too?" Cardinal did. He sang and sang, and Daisy imagined that he was telling her about the fine feast he would eat that day, and about the angels in the trees and had she seen St. Joseph? He was a friend of birds. He had flown into Egypt.

"How's my Bird Girl this morning?" Mom asked from the door.

Daisy pointed to the mockingbird from among the paper birds she had taped to her ceiling above her top bunk.

"A mockingbird? Hmm. Tell me about that," Mom said. She began to lay out fresh clothes over Daisy's chair.

"I'm listening."

"To the cardinal?"

"Yes. He says he likes St. Joseph because he flew into Egypt."

"That he did," Mom smiled. She stood on tiptoe and kissed Daisy's forehead. "I've put your clothes out for you. You can follow Sunday schedule this

49

morning since we have Divine Liturgy." Mom pointed to the wall over Daisy's low white bookcase, where a series of pictures showed each part of the Sunday morning routine.

"Thank you, Mommy." Daisy yawned and sat up all the way in bed.

"I love you, Daisy," Mom said. Then she shut the door before Georgy and Nicky and Rosie could invade Daisy's morning routine. Daisy could hear Mom through the door, telling the babies about the plates of toast downstairs. "Toast!" the babies echoed. Daisy waited till their little footsteps subsided down the stairs before she kissed her icons of the Theotokos and St. Anastasia, made her cross, and climbed down from her bed.

Daddy had gone early to church to help chant the prayers before Divine Liturgy, so Daisy was in charge of Rosie till everyone got to the pew. Gabe held the door for the family so Mommy could walk in holding Nicky and Georgy's hands. Rosie's little hand was plump and wiggly, and Daisy had to reach out with both hands to keep hold of her. Rosie rushed in ahead and pulled Daisy behind her. As soon as they were inside, Rosie jumped and grabbed Daisy around the waist and buried her head in Daisy's tummy. Daisy grimaced and took deep breaths till she could feel her belly move again. She patted Rosie's head.

"What is it, Rosie?" Daisy asked.

"A dwagon!" Rosie cried.

Daisy pulled herself out of Rosie's grip and knelt till her baby sister's eyes were above hers. "It's okay, Rosie." Daisy said in a soft voice. "Look what God has done." She pointed to the icon, and Rosie's gaze followed. Rosie hugged Daisy's side and trembled. "Don't worry, Rosie," Daisy said, and the air around them shimmered, "Be brave and look with me. There's a surprise in the painting." Rosie loved surprises, and she followed Daisy to look closer. "See? The icon makes the dragon small enough for you to step on."

Rosie giggled. "I smash him like a bug!" She laughed. Daisy smiled. The air around them softened.

"Where's bug, Rosie?" Georgy asked.

"In your hair!" Nicky giggled.

Georgy rubbed his head. "It not. You have bugs in your hair!"

Mom's face reddened, and she knelt by the twins. "No one has any bugs in their hair. Now, boys, let's light your candles and kiss the icons."

"I smash dwagon like bug!" Rosie said to the twins.

Mom looked hard at the twins, who were turning their heads to glance between the icon of St. George and the dragon and Rosie's shoe with great interest. "Oh, no, you don't!" Mom said, grabbing them by the hands and tugging them towards the door to the nave. "You may not step on an icon."

Rosie looked up at Daisy when the twins and Mom had gone into the main part of the church. "I squish dwagon now?"

"For pretend. Pretend he's there," Daisy pointed to a spot on the floor. "And stomp on him."

Rosie stomped.

Gabe handed Daisy a candle. "The dragon represents our sinful appetites and bad habits that consume us if we feed them instead of submitting to Christ."

"I know," Daisy said. "But Rosie's only little."

"What does he say?" Gabe asked in a whisper, nodding toward the icon of St. George.

Daisy listened. She heard Rosie stomping, Dad and Father chanting the end of the morning prayer service before Liturgy, men's voices in the hallway trying not to be overheard, the comfortable clatter of candles in the box, St. Anastasia praying for her from the window of her icon with echoes of scripture, "power, love, and a sound mind,…righteousness, peace, and joy in the Holy Spirit," and nearer, but quietly, the low thrum of St. George's voice, "Love is brave. May the love of Christ be with you."

"Love of Christ be with you. Love is brave," Daisy repeated to Gabe. She smiled as she heard an answer in her own heart. "Be of good cheer, Gabe," she said, "for Christ has overcome the world."

Gabe smiled, nodded, and looked around. "Where's Rosie?"

They found her under the icon stand, where she had wedged herself into the narrow space and sat down.

"What are you doing, Rosie?" Daisy asked.

"Taking off my shoe."

"How about we wait till we get home, and I'll draw you a dragon to squish?" Daisy asked.

"Scawy dwagon?"

"I'll make you a scary one," Gabe replied, "and Daisy will make you a pretty one." He turned to Daisy. "No offense, Sis, but all of your drawings are cute."

Daisy nodded. He was right.

They finished kissing the icons and lighting their candles, and Gabe led the way to their seats.

Daisy thought of her friends in their nest all through the Kyrie eleisons. She almost forgot about sorting her seeds, until she saw two agents walking along the far aisle during the, "Holy, holy, holy." She grabbed her seeds and went to the away room at the back of the church. The door was locked. She shook her head and wondered what to do next.

She took three deep breaths. Dad must have locked the door. Maybe the girls were safe. Maybe she could go back to her seat.

"Can I help you with something, little girl?" a deep voice spoke right by her ear, startling her.

Daisy screamed and dropped her bag. The man who had startled her, one of the strange agents, stepped back, alarmed. Ms. Elena came up to her from the pews and took her hand.

"Come on, Daisy," Ms. Elena said. Her voice was gentle, but she glared at the man. "I'll find you a place." They walked through the narthex to the hallway leading towards the classrooms. "How about under this tablecloth?" Ms. Elena asked, lifting the cloth on a table covered with icons and photographs. "It's nice and dim, and you can step right back into the service when you're ready." Ms. Elena bent over as Daisy crawled into the space under the table. "The girls are safe for today," she whispered. "You just take care of yourself, and then you can go into communion."

Daisy nodded and sniffled. Ms. Elena dropped the cloth into place, and Daisy opened her sorting board. She gave "startled," "overwhelmed," and "scared" to Jesus to redeem. Then she stopped to listen to herself. She had almost deciphered whether she was relieved or hopeful about the little girls upstairs, when she heard someone speaking nearby. It was the same men's voices she had noticed when she was listening for St. George earlier. They were coming from just around the corner in the hallway, and now she could hear them clearly.

"Was that the little retarded girl screaming?" one voice asked. It sounded like the man that Mom had bossed before church the day before.

"I don't think she's retarded. I think she's up to something. I scared her, and some lady took her off somewhere."

It was the agents! She had to be quiet under the table, or they might find her. Daisy took three slow, steady breaths and found the little "help" hand in her bunch of seeds. She touched it to the Cross and to Panagia's veil. "Help me, Theotokos!" she prayed, moving her lips without sound. "Help me, Lord Jesus!"

The man who had startled her spoke again. "I found their church directory and got on their listserv. This Jocelyne Smith is a relative. What do you say we pay her a visit at her house this Friday night?"

"Why Friday? Think you'll find the Georges there because it's a weekend? They got away from you on a weekend in the first place. I doubt they're going to stick around someplace so obvious."

"The Georges are troublemakers, Jim. But you're right. They're probably not going to be home. There's plenty of troublemakers to choose from here, though."

"I don't know, Carl," the man from the narthex, Jim, said. "I think we should drop it." From her hiding spot under the table, Daisy could not see the saints around him, but she heard them urging him to do justly. "Why are you so interested in catching this family anyway?"

"They come over here, " Carl the mean agent began. His voice sounded angry, and he sucked his teeth instead of finishing his sentence. Daisy felt sad for him and put "sad" on the Cross. Agent Carl reminded her of a wolf she'd read about in her book of Aesop's Fables, but she didn't quite recall what the moral of that fable had been.

"I don't know, man. I served in Iraq and Afghanistan to protect our values. I want people to come here for safety if they can't find refuge elsewhere." Daisy could hear the murmur of the warrior saints around Agent Jim, giving him courage and reminding him of why he had fought.

Agent Carl didn't seem to hear the saints. His voice reminded her of the dark and scaly dragon like the one St. George had slain. "Well, maybe I just don't like that woman. Why did she elbow me in the chest and run when I stopped her? That ain't freedom. That ain't refugee behavior. That's guilt when you run away like that."

"I don't know, Carl. I've seen some of these places. You think everyone's an enemy when the sky is falling." Daisy shook her head and remembered Hannan's words. Her friends had run from a falling sky, a world blown to shreds. She patted the Cross, where she would have added sadness if it were not already there.

Agent Carl scoffed as though he'd tasted vinegar and hot peppers.

"Naw, man," Agent Jim soothed. "These aren't troublemakers."

"They're all the same." Agent Carl's voice sounded muffled to Daisy, as though he were coiling in on himself, clinging tighter and tighter to a lie. Suddenly she remembered what it was about the wolf in that fable that reminded her of Agent Carl. Any excuse will do for a tyrant. She shuddered and tapped her "help" hand on her sorting board.

"If it was up to me," Agent Jim responded calmly, "I'd say let's leave this church and these people alone. You know it's going to scare the Dickens out of those little kids if we detain them. Not to mention the parents."

"Well, it ain't up to you, Jim. We're going to pay the Costas family a little visit tonight and see if they're less antagonistic after Grandma spends the night in detention. Then we'll track down this

Jocelyne person and see if she leads us to the Georges."

Daisy sat forward and covered her mouth with her hand. Her Nouna's family name was Costas. Nouna was a lawyer. Maybe she had been irritating the agents, and now they were going to steal Nouna's mother-in-law out of their house. Daisy needed to tell Nouna Marina right away. She listened hard to see if the coast was clear, but the men's voices had fallen silent.

Just then, Ms. Elena lifted the edge of the tablecloth. "Are you ready to go to communion?"

"Yes. I want to go with my Nouna. Is she here?" Daisy scrambled out from under the table and pulled her seed folder with her.

Agent Carl glowered and took a step toward her from around the corner, but Agent Jim stopped him with an arm across his chest. Daisy blinked at Agent Jim, and he nodded at her. She turned and walked into the nave with Ms. Elena.

In the church, everyone was saying the prayer before communion together. Daisy could hear Nouna Marina's voice booming over everyone else's. Daisy followed the sound and joined her at the line that made no sense. "Unworthy as I am, how can I enter the splendor of the company of your saints?" It was a "well-intentioned" prayer – Mom had taught her that phrase to describe how sometimes people could mean well and still not make sense – but the fact was that saints didn't bother with worthiness. Saints came to people who asked for help, not people who did everything right.

Under the boom of Nouna's voice, Daisy asked the saints for help now. Immediately, she heard St. Anastasia beside her. "Be of good cheer. Christ is the victor," she heard as in an echo. It was one of the truths Anastasias told, that Christ wins. She knew it, too, though she used less old-fashioned words to say it. Christ wins over death. Christ wins our hearts in love. Like a whisper and a flame by her ear, she heard

St. Anastasia say, "I will stand between you and danger for Christ's sake." Daisy turned her face upward toward the saint and nodded.

St. Anastasia had made Daisy brave, and she took Nouna's hand and tugged. Nouna smiled down at her and leaned over. Daisy whispered in her ear, "The agents are going to come pester your family tonight so the church will give them our friends."

"Oh, are they?" Nouna raised one eyebrow and stood upright. She was formidable even though she was only a head taller than Daisy. "We'll see about that." Then Daisy was surrounded by the crisp, fruity green of Nouna's fragrance as she hugged her to her side. "You're my brave goddaughter." She kissed the top of Daisy's head. "Let's go to communion so we have strength for what's ahead." Around them, the air was bright with the company of heaven and the susurrus of saints egging them on. "Courage," they said, and "Christ is victor," and "Xristos nika," which means the same. Daisy opened her mouth and ate the love that gave her the courage and the victory, too.

***

That evening, Mom came to tuck Daisy in for the night. "I have news from your Nouna," she said. "Her mother-in-law and aunt are visiting the monastery this week to ask Panagia's help. They weren't home when the agents came to call."

"Will they be safe there?" Daisy asked.

"I think so. So far the agents don't seem to know where the monastery is, and they don't have jurisdiction there, anyway. Not that the church is their jurisdiction, either, but the monastery is too far from the seashore to give them an excuse to search."

"Will Nour and Hannan and Mary have to go there, too?" Now that Daisy had found her friends, she didn't like the idea of them moving far away.

"Maybe. But I think we can keep them safe here in the city if we get everything we need in one place."

"Mom, am I retarded?"

"No, Daisy." Her mother frowned. "Where did you hear that?"

"The agents called me that."

"Oh, my Bird Girl, I'm so sorry. Even if you had a cognitive delay, which is the kind way to talk about people whose brains don't develop as much as the rest of them, even then you would be beyond priceless and so loved and a joy to me. Those men who said that have tried to tape their broken hearts back together with unkindness instead of letting the broken parts be a path for healing to flow through." Daisy imagined the men with duct tape on their chests, drowning in water that was meant to wash them and make them float. It didn't make sense, so she looked toward the icon of the Theotokos. Beside mother, Panagia brightened the air like roses, whispering, "A sword shall pierce your own heart, too."

"Panagia's heart was pierced with sorrow," Daisy said.

"Yes, Daisy, and her compassion and love show us how to treat wounded people."

"Even the mean ones?"

"Even the mean ones."

Daisy turned and looked at the icon of the Theotokos again. In her nous-heart she heard the sound of Mary's song, "for He has regarded the lowliness of His handmaiden."

Daisy looked back to Mom.

"You have a flame in your eyes tonight," Mom said. She walked across the room and turned off the lamp. "Ask God to keep it while you sleep." She kissed Daisy's forehead. "You need to get some rest."

Daisy nodded.

When Mom left, Daisy opened her mind to God. She thought of Nour with inside eyes and Cooey whose eyes remembered the sky and Agent Carl who had seen the sky fall. She listened to the Theotokos' words echo in the dark, "the lowliness of His handmaiden," and she began to pray.

She was as low to the ground as a beetle, then rising on wings above trees and danger, then tucked small into a pocket of Panagia's robes, then singing as loud as the angels who call Panagia their joy. She tumbled through small and large and quiet and loud and safe and exposed until her heart caught on a little spoon that fed her fire and love.

Her breath filled with sweetness, and she saw the Lord in a brief instance, the hand coming to rest on her head and His smile as He blessed the children. Nour was beside her, smiling up at Him with eyes reflecting the uncreated sun.

She was pulled back suddenly to her bed, and as she fell out of the vision, she saw the multitudes of children of every size and shape and color, some with missing limbs or teeth or eyes, all smiling up at Him as He placed His hands on their heads. Each of them was as near to Him as she and Nour had been, though she could not see the edges of the multitude.

"Let them come to me," she heard, and she fell asleep in perfect peace. Her bed was a nest on the Tree of the Cross, and Nour and Hannan and Mary were tucked there, too. Downstairs, Cooey sang. In the dream nest, Cooey tucked his head under his wing beside Nour. Daisy slipped beyond dreaming just as two pairs of wings settled over them. In her sleep, she whispered, "And with two, they flew."

# eight

The following Sunday dawned to the song of two cardinals at Daisy's window. Daisy sat up in bed and waved to the chirruping pair. Behind them, angels and a few Stylite saints sat singing hymns in the trees. She waved at them, too.

Daisy dressed quickly and went to Cooey's cage. Cooey pushed against the bars.

"You want out so early?" Daisy asked. She looked around the living room. No one else was up yet, though she could hear the shower running in Mom and Dad's bathroom. "Okay. We have time." She opened the latch and lifted the door.

Cooey poked out his head, tilted it side to side to get the shape of things, and hopped out onto Daisy's hand. She lifted him in her open palm and petted his soft head. With a sudden flurry, Cooey flew into the air. His lopsided wings wouldn't let him go far, but he circled above Daisy's head twice before lighting on top of his cage.

"Did you wear yourself out already?" Daisy asked him. "You have to work harder than other birds to fly, but look! You did it."

Cooey answered her by fluffing the feathers on his partial wing. Then he cooed loudly.

Daisy nodded at him. "I understand. I have to work harder, too. But I'm still a girl, and you're still a dove. We know more about mercy, is all. We can't do anything without eleison."

"Daisy?" Mom asked from the doorway. Her head was wrapped in a towel, and her bare feet showed under her long, spring church dress. "You're up early. Would you like some toast?"

"Good morning, Mom. I would like some toast, but I have to watch Cooey."

"How about I watch Cooey, and you make some toast?" Mom asked. Daisy thought about the question for a few seconds. Usually Mom made the toast, but lately she'd been changing small parts of their routine to help Daisy adjust her expectations and know that little changes are safe. Mom hadn't said as much to Daisy, but Daisy saw the pattern between the books she studied in speech therapy and lessons Mom tried to teach around the house.

"Okay, Mommy. I can be flexible."

Mom smiled. "Thank you, Daisy."

After Daisy and the other children had finished their Sunday breakfast of toast with honey and cups of pear juice, she went to her room to finish getting ready for church. She tried to remember the feeling of her dream from the night before. When the feeling came back to her, she was looking at the little icon of the Theotokos of Vladimir that she kept on her bookshelf.

Usually, she thought of the little icon like a window that helped to light her bedroom with God's love. This morning, it reminded her of the safe feeling of being in the nest on the Cross with the other bird girls. She decided to take it to Mary, Hannan, and Nour so that they could have the feeling with them, too. She placed the icon into her church bag along with the seed-sorting folder.

When they arrived at church, they had to park far away from the sidewalk. Usually they had several spots to choose from when they arrived just before Liturgy. Most families with small children trickled into the service between the end of the Doxology and the Small Entrance. Today was different. Today there was a crowd like the church usually only had at Pascha.

Daisy had to take three deep breaths to calm down from all the bustling, muscling people waiting to venerate the icons in the narthex. She could hear St. Anastasia through the small noises of the moving people, but she couldn't linger at her icon. Mom was right beside her, holding Rosie's hand in one hand and hastily lighting candles with the other.

"Let's get to our seats, Daisy," Mom said.

She tried to move away from the icon of St. Anastasia, but the bustle and noise and the unexpected crowd were interrupting Daisy's thoughts. She could feel herself losing touch with her feet and the world around her. Her body felt cold, and she wasn't sure what to do. She glanced at her hands, and she was surprised to see that she was still holding her church bag. In the depths of the bag, she could see the little icon of the Theotokos. She remembered what she needed to do.

"Can I go straight to my seeds, Mommy?" Daisy asked. She looked around at the people and the flame-soaked air. For a moment, she could smell the beeswax and hear the angel song that drove off fear. Then she started to freeze again, her body following her thoughts. Mom looked worried and knelt down beside Daisy, bringing warmth with her.

"Yes, Daisy." Mom cupped Daisy's cheek in her hand and kissed her forehead. "Oh, my little Bird Girl. Today is so much for you. Yes, go and sort your seeds." Mom took Daisy's hand and walked her to the away room at the back of the nave before Mom and Rosie continued on to where the family sat with the rest of the Sunday school families.

Daisy looked around the crowded room. If there were agents there, she couldn't see them. She opened the door and went in. The room was dim and a little quieter than the rest of the church. It held the smell of incense the same way as her church dresses in her closet at home. The smell was a remembering smell.

She could collect herself in it and go back to the source when the time was right.

Daisy pulled out the sorting folder and opened it on the soft rug under the window. She laid out the seeds all around the folder, but she didn't sort them. That could come later. First, she needed to take the little icon to her friends. She lifted the icon, kissed it, and held it against her chest. She found the tiny seam of the hidden door and pried it open with her fingernails. The scent of rose water puffed out and surrounded her. She slipped into the hidden staircase and pulled the door closed behind her.

"It's you," Hannan said from above her. The light wasn't as bright this Sunday, and Daisy blinked a few times until her eyes adjusted enough to see the little girl's bright, dark eyes in the blotchy colors from the stained-glass window.

"Hi, Hannan," Daisy waved. "I brought you something. It helped us in a dream." She walked up the stairs and held out the icon. Hannan took it and stared at it.

"Kiss it," Nour said, coming forward from the shadows of the corner where she had been sitting.

"Let me see," Mary bossed. She took the icon from Hannan's hands, firmly but reverently. She kissed it and smiled. "This is the snake stomping icon!" she said to her sisters.

"What do you mean?" Daisy asked, thinking of the dragon from the feast last week. She looked over Hannan's shoulder to make sure that she had not somehow given the wrong icon or that the icon had not somehow changed.

"Have you ever seen a snake about to strike?" Hannan asked. "Look! Look at the tilt of Panagia's head."

Daisy looked at the Theotokos' head, leaning over to cuddle baby Jesus. She shook her head, not sure what the girls meant.

"Tell her, Nour," Hannan continued. "You're the one who noticed it."

"I saw a snake one time," Nour said, her big eyes conveying the feelings of the story so that Daisy was a little afraid, too. "It was about to bite Mary, but I saw it before she stepped on it. I told her to stop, and the snake didn't bite. But it tilted its head at her just like the angle of Theotokos' head. Only, she is the opposite of the snake. She crushed the snake's head. She undid the sin from the snake's temptation."

Daisy reached out and touched the icon. She could see what Nour meant. It was an icon that set wrong things right. "Last night I was praying with this icon when I saw us all safe in a nest on the Cross."

Nour smiled, and Hannan and Mary passed the icon between them.

"It's our family's favorite," Mary said. "Thank you for bringing it."

"What else did you bring?" Nour asked.

Daisy stared at her for a moment, embarrassed that she did not have another gift for her friends.

"Don't be rude," Mary said. "She's so kind to think of us, and Panagia told her to bring the icon. That's special."

"I mean words. She has words in her heart to tell us." Nour looked at Daisy expectantly, and Daisy remembered.

"Right before I went to the other part of sleep, I heard some words. 'And with two they flew.'" She looked to each of the other girls. Mary shrugged, and Hannan shook her head. "It's about the wings of the seraphim. With two they covered their faces, with two they covered their feet, and with two they flew." Daisy looked at Nour. Nour nodded. "It was a good feeling when I heard it. A safe feeling."

"Thank you," Mary said. Daisy could tell the words didn't mean anything to her, but Daisy felt lighter, having said them.

"Come sit with us," Hannan said. She gestured toward the cushions where the girls had been resting. The girls started toward them, but they were interrupted by a gruff voice from below.

"I told you that girl was up to something!" Agent Carl said. He sounded angry. "Her stuff's in here, but where's she? Look in that closet."

Other voices joined him. "What's going on in here?" one of the ushers asked. The response was drowned out by Ms. Jocelyne's voice, shouting at Agent Carl to get out of the church. Agent Carl yelled back that he had a duty to be there. Daisy looked at the other little girls, each of them wide-eyed. Hannan covered her mouth, and Nour clung to Mary's side. Daisy ran down the stairs to grab the knob of the door to hold it shut. It would be a terrible time for the wind to pull it open.

People were opening and closing the outer door of the away room, shouting at each other all the while. They created suction. Just as Daisy reached the bottom step, the door creaked open a centimeter.

She was too late.

She froze. Maybe no one would see.

But the room on the other side of the door had gone quiet. Suddenly, the door was yanked open, and Agent Carl's massive shoulders filled the small doorway. Daisy saw the fire of angel wings all around her, and she knew what she had to do.

"Run!" she yelled up at her friends. Then, as loudly as she could, she screamed at Agent Carl. "Get away!" Her ears throbbed with the sound, and she did not know how many times she screamed. All she knew was that Agent Carl covered his ears and backed up in shock, and Hannan ran out of the doorway behind her to the safety of her Aunt Jocelyne's arms. Men and women came into the room around them and joined her in telling the agent to leave. The sounds of their voices and the fire of the angel wings beat him back toward the window.

Suddenly, Daisy realized that he was stepping on her seed-sorting folder. She paused to look down at it. In the sudden quiet, Agent Carl sprang toward the door, knocking Daisy back through the doorway with him. She grabbed his leg to keep him from going up the stairs. He looked down at her in disgust, and for a moment she thought he was going to kick her. There was a noise from above them. They both looked up as Mary lost her grip on a terrified Nour.

Daisy lifted her arms toward her friend in a prayer like the Mother of God holding out her scarf. In the same moment, Nour flew. She didn't fall down the stairs, though the adults might have seen it like that if they had been watching. Only Daisy and Nour saw what really happened. An angel covered Nour's head and feet with two sets of wings, and with two, they flew. Nour flew over the staircase and landed on Agent Carl's chest, knocking him flat on his back through the door. Nour and Daisy scrambled up, uninjured. Agent Carl shook his head and stood up.

The "confused" seed stuck to the back of his head by his collar.

Nour and Daisy saw it and started to laugh. They were cut short by Nouna Marina's loud voice.

"Let me through!" she demanded, and the people parted, pulling Daisy and Nour out of the way and into the safety of many mothers and fathers. Nouna stood in front of Agent Carl like a strong pillar, though she was a foot and a half shorter than him even in her high heels. She held out a stack of white papers backed with a blue paper. "Restraining order," she said. "Get. Out." She didn't yell, but for the first time, Agent Carl nodded and made to leave.

The people parted and quieted as Agent Carl left the church. Daisy could hear the chanters singing a long responsive psalm. Father must have told them to do the longer version of the readings so the service could continue during the excitement. She looked around for Nour and held her hand. Nour smiled.

Suddenly, they were both pulled into the tree-scented world of Nouna's hug.

"Look at my brave girls," Nouna boomed over them. "Let's get these girls back into church." She walked them to the doorway. "Come on, Hannan, Mary. You girls are all sitting with me and my goddaughter today."

At the end of the service, instead of Sunday school, there was a parish meeting. Everyone had pastries and coffee while the young doctor from the Society of St. Philaret meeting told them the plan. The George family needed to get away from the church without being stopped. That was the reason for the Pascha-sized crowd. Everyone would leave together, but three families would each take one of the girls in their cars. They were to head to the monastery in the western part of the state, where the family would be reunited and have their papers and court documents restored to them. Then, all the families would come back to town safely.

Daisy sat at a table with Nour and Hannan and Mary and Natalyia, coloring an image of the Myrrh-Bearing Women. She didn't look up when the speakers changed until Nouna Marina got up to speak. Nouna told the people about how Daisy and Nour took down the mean agent. Everybody clapped. Daisy and Nour covered their ears. They looked at each other and smiled.

# nine

The following Saturday, Daisy woke up early and cleaned her room. She lined her toys up neatly along her table and the walls. She placed her books in the bookshelf. She dusted the little shelf of icons. Mom had given her another icon of the Theotokos to replace the one that Daisy had given to Mary, Hannan, and Nour. It was smaller than the one she had given to the girls, and there was extra room on the shelf. Daisy lined up the icons the way she always had. She left a gap at the end of the row instead of spreading them out to take up the whole space. Icons looked cozier together, and Daisy liked knowing where to find them when she reached for them.

Around lunchtime, there was a knock at the door. Daisy ran downstairs to see who it was. Mom opened the door and immediately reached out to hug the dark-haired woman on the front stoop.

"Susan!" Mom said, pulling back so that Daisy could see that the woman wore a sling on her left arm, "I'm so glad to see you." She wiped tears from her eyes and stepped backward, gesturing the woman in. "Come in, come in," Mom said.

Ms. Susan stepped in, and Nour stepped in right behind her. Nour looked around and saw Daisy right away. Daisy ran up to her.

"Come on, Nour," Daisy said, taking her hand. "I want you to meet my bird."

The girls walked together to the large cage on the far side of the living room. Mom and Nour's mom,

Ms. Susan, closed the door and went towards the kitchen. The twins and Rosie followed, asking loud questions about the cast on Ms. Susan's arm. Daisy watched the little procession till they were out of the room. Then she turned to the cage.

"Cooey," Daisy said, "This is Nour. She has sky eyes like you." Cooey fluttered to the perch by the door to the cage and waited.

"Nour," Daisy said, "This is Cooey. He understands bird girls." Nour looked at Cooey and smiled with her big, deep eyes. "Would you like to pet him?" Daisy asked.

Nour nodded.

Daisy opened the cage and held out her palm. Cooey hopped onto her hand and lowered his head so that Daisy could lift him safely out of the cage. She held him close and kissed his head. She whispered, "Nour can fly, too." She cupped Cooey in her hands and held him toward Nour. "Go ahead and touch his head if you'd like."

Nour stroked his head and neck with one finger. "I wasn't the one flying," Nour said.

Cooey nodded his head and cooed. Nour jumped at the loud sound. Daisy giggled.

"He likes you," Daisy said.

Warm smells wafted into the living room: chicken and saffron rice and pitas and tomato sauce and coffee and baklava with nuts. Mom and Ms. Susan came to the doorway from the kitchen. "Girls," Mom said, "Put Cooey away for a little while and come wash your hands for lunch."

The girls nodded. Daisy returned Cooey to his perch inside the cage. Nour skipped to her mother's side and said something in a low voice. When Daisy turned around, she saw Nour waiting for her by the kitchen door.

"I want to give you something," Nour said. She held out a small, hand-painted wooden plaque covered in reds and gold leaf. "It's a seraphim. My dad painted it."

Daisy took the icon into her hands and turned it so that the light flashed on it. It was as close as paint and gold could get to the fire of the angel wings that filled the church and followed the girls. "Thank you," Daisy said.

"Girls, hands," Mom said from where she dished out food by the stove. Nour went to her mother, but Daisy ran toward the stairs.

"Be right back, Mommy!" she called. She ran to her room and placed the little seraphim alongside the other icons on her shelf. It fit perfectly, snug as a bird in a nest. She could hear singing from the other side of it. "Holy, holy, holy!" it sang, and Daisy leaned her head over to hear the whole world echo God's glory.

"Daisy," Mom said from the door, "What's keeping you? Come wash your hands and join us for dinner. We have guests."

Daisy looked from Mom to the icon shelf. Mom came alongside her and looked with her. "Just like you," Mom said, and she touched the golden edge of the seraphim. "You sing holy and hear holy in God's whole world." Mom made her cross, kissed the icons, and then kissed the top of Daisy's head.

Daisy stood on her tiptoes and fluttered her fingers.

"I love you, my little Bird Girl."

The End

# About the Author

Catherine Bodega is an autistic bookworm who lives in North Carolina in the company of her holy icons and three goofy birds. Her Orthodox Christian faith and love for everyone God has made help her filter the news of the world. She wrote this story for all the autistic little girls who are always underestimated.

# About Park End Books

Park End Books is a traditional small press bringing to market accessible curricula and emerging Catholic, Orthodox, and other creedal Christian authors. Visit us online at ParkEndBooks.com.

### Coming Soon:

*Our Autistic Home* by Summer Kinard

Learn how to make your household into a place where autistic family members thrive. Kinard brings the wisdom garnered from life in an all-autistic household to help families plan, adapt, understand, and remove handicaps to autistic functioning so that everyone feels truly at home. With the easy to apply tips and resources in this book, you can start a new era of joy for your entire family.

*Letters for Pilgrimage: Lenten Meditations for Teen Girls* by Sarah Lenora Gingrich and A.N. Tallent (February 2021)

These seven weeks of letters engage the imagination and anchor the senses in stories that help awaken faith for teens on the Lenten journey. Evocative linocut illustrations by noted artist Ned Bustard pair with each week to draw hearts to attention to life with God in our every circumstance.

**PARK END BOOKS**